CLASSIC STARTS™

Around the World in 80 Days

*Retold from the Jules Verne original
by Deanna McFadden*

Illustrated by Jamel Akib

Sterling Publishing Co., Inc.
New York

Library of Congress Cataloging-in-Publication Data

McFadden, Deanna.
   Around the world in 80 days / adapted from the Jules Verne original by
Deanna McFadden ; illustrated by Jamel Akib ; afterword by Arthur Pober.
      p. cm.—(Classic starts)
   Summary: In 1872, English gentleman Phileas Fogg has many adventures as
he tries to win a bet that he can travel around the world in eighty days.
   ISBN-13: 978-1-4027-3689-6
   ISBN-10: 1-4027-3689-4
   [1. Voyages around the world—Fiction. 2. Adventure and adventurers—
Fiction.] I. Akib, Jamel, ill. II. Pober, Arthur. III. Verne, Jules, 1828–1905. Tour
du monde en quatre-vingts jours. English. IV. Title. V. Title: Around the world
in eighty days. VI. Series.

PZ7.M4784548Ar 2007
[Fic]—dc22
                                                                        2006014519

                        2 4 6 8 10 9 7 5 3 1

                    Published by Sterling Publishing Co., Inc.
                   387 Park Avenue South, New York, NY 10016
                       Copyright © 2007 by Deanna McFadden
                     Illustrations copyright © 2007 by Jamel Akib
                     ᶜ/ₒ Canadian Manda Group, 165 Dufferin Street
                        Toronto, Ontario, Canada M6K 3H6
              Distributed in the United Kingdom by GMC Distribution Services,
         Castle Place, 166 High Street, Lewes, East Sussex, England BN7 1XU
              Distributed in Australia by Capricorn Link (Australia) Pty. Ltd.
                      P.O. Box 704, Windsor, NSW 2756, Australia

            Classic Starts is a trademark of Sterling Publishing Co., Inc.

                    Sterling ISBN-13: 978-1-4027-3689-6
                         ISBN-10: 1-4027-3689-4

          For information about custom editions, special sales, premium and
                corporate purchases, please contact Sterling Special Sales
             Department at 800-805-5489 or specialsales@sterlingpub.com.

Contents

CHAPTER 1

Phileas Fogg Finds a New Butler

Mr. Phileas Fogg lived at No. 7 Savile Row in London, England. Long ago, a famous poet had lived in his house. Some people said he looked like the poet, but they weren't related. Phileas was a tall man with dark hair and a serious face. On his last birthday, he had turned forty and his hair and whiskers had started to turn gray. Other than what he looked like and the fact that he was wealthy, no one knew much about Phileas Fogg.

With the exception of his butler, Phileas lived alone in the house on Savile Row. When he wasn't at home, he could usually be found at the Reform Club. This was where he ate most of his meals. With the master of the house away for so much of the day, the butler did not have a long list of everyday duties. But his small list was important.

Phileas Fogg was very particular about how he wanted things done. They had to be done exactly right. In fact, just this morning he had fired his butler, James Forster, for bringing him shaving water that was two degrees too cold!

Now Phileas was sitting in an armchair in his living room. He was waiting for his new butler to arrive. There was a strange clock in a corner of the room. It showed the hours, the minutes, the seconds, the days, the months, and the years. Phileas timed his life by this clock. It was quite a sight when all the hands on the clock moved at once.

It was just a few minutes before eleven-thirty. At precisely eleven-thirty, Phileas would leave for the Reform Club. There was a knock at the door and James stepped inside. He had just finished packing and was on his way out the door.

He said, "The new butler, sir." Then he turned on his heel and left the room.

A young man of about thirty stepped forward and bowed. "My name is Jean Passepartout," he said.

"What time is it?" Phileas asked.

Passepartout pulled out his pocket watch and looked at it carefully. "Twenty-two minutes after eleven, sir," he said.

"Your watch is slow," Phileas replied.

"Pardon me, monsieur, but that is impossible—"

"Your watch is four minutes too slow," Phileas repeated. "Very well. From this very

moment, eleven twenty-six on Wednesday, October 2, 1867, you are now my butler."

With that said, Phileas Fogg got up from his chair, put on his hat, and left.

⌒

The sound of the closing door echoed through the empty halls. "Faith!" Passepartout whispered to himself. "I've seen figures at Madame Tussauds Wax Museum that are livelier than my new boss!"

Passepartout had been searching for the perfect place to work since leaving Paris five years earlier. When he learned that Phileas Fogg was looking for a new butler, he jumped at the chance to work for him. He knew Mr. Fogg was a man who liked things a certain way and Passepartout was looking for a good, solid routine. In fact, what Passepartout wanted above all else was an orderly life.

As he stepped out of the sitting room and into

the hallway, he thought about what had just happened. It would be hard to know how he and Mr. Fogg would get along from that short meeting. *Will I be able to do this job just as he wants me to?* Passepartout wondered.

Passepartout set off to explore the house from top to bottom. What he found was a house that was so clean it shined. Everything had a place! While looking around on the second floor, he came upon his own bedroom. There were electric bells and long speaking tubes to help him keep in touch with the lower floors. And there was an electric clock on the mantelpiece. It was just like the one in Mr. Fogg's living room. It even kept the exact same time.

"This will do!" Passepartout said. "This will do!"

He glanced over at the clock and noticed a piece of paper hanging on the wall. It was the schedule for all of his chores.

Perfect! Passepartout thought. *Now I can learn the routine as well.*

The entire day was planned. Phileas Fogg woke up at precisely eight o'clock in the morning. Breakfast was to be brought to him exactly twenty-three minutes later. At nine thirty-seven he liked to shave. Passepartout knew what he should be doing every second of every day. In fact, there was a system for everything! Even Mr. Fogg's clothes and shoes were numbered according to when they were worn, whether summer or fall.

Having seen the house from top to bottom, Passepartout said aloud, "We'll get along just fine, Mr. Fogg and I. This is just what I wanted!"

CHAPTER 2

Phileas Fogg Says Something He Might Regret

⌒ↄ

Phileas Fogg left his house and walked the five hundred and seventy-five steps to the Reform Club. He went straight to the dining room and sat down at his usual table. Just outside the dining room was a garden that he liked to look at. Phileas's usual waiter brought him his usual lunch, which, as usual, he finished at precisely twelve forty-seven.

After lunch, Phileas moved into the great hall to read the papers. He spent much of the day there and then went back into the dining room for his supper. When he finished eating, he sat in the Reading Room with some other members of the club. At ten past six, he started playing cards with his friends.

Among Phileas's friends were Andrew Stuart, an engineer, and Thomas Flanagan, a landowner. John Sullivan and Samuel Fallentin were also there. They both owned newspapers. Lastly there was Ralph Gauthier, who worked for the Bank of England. Everyone wanted to hear about the robbery that had taken place at the bank just three days ago. The robber had gotten away with a fortune of fifty-five thousand pounds. It had been all over the papers.

"Shall we get started, gentlemen?" John Sullivan asked. "I am looking forward to picking up our game of bridge."

They discussed who was to deal and then

started playing cards. As each man settled into the game, Thomas Flanagan asked, "Well, Ralph, what do you think about that robbery?"

"The bank will certainly lose the money!" Andrew Stuart cut in.

"On the contrary," Ralph said, "I think we'll be able to catch the robber! We've sent detectives across the country and to the four corners of the world. He won't slip through our fingers."

"So you know what he looks like, then?" Andrew asked.

"He's no regular robber, that's for sure," Ralph replied.

"He made off with so much money! What do you mean he's not a regular robber?!" Andrew laughed.

"He's a gentleman. At least that's what the papers are saying," Ralph responded.

Ralph told the group that a number of people had seen a well-dressed gentleman in the very room where the money went missing. This had been on the same day that it was stolen. The police were convinced that it was this gentleman who had committed the crime, for no one else had been seen in the room. Ralph also told the men that the bank had offered a reward to the detective who managed to catch the thief. It was a very good reward, too—two thousand pounds!

"Where do you think he'll go then, if you've got men all around the world?" Andrew asked.

"Oh, the world is quite big enough to hide one smart fellow," Thomas said.

"It used to be," Phileas said as he dealt the cards around the table.

"What do you mean?" Andrew asked. "Has the world grown smaller?"

"Absolutely!" Ralph said. "I agree with Phileas. A man can travel so much faster these days. That is exactly why we're going to catch the thief. We can keep one step ahead of him by having detectives in any corner of the world where he might be hiding."

"Ah," Andrew said, "but it's also how the thief could get away."

"Perhaps, but that doesn't change the fact that one man can now travel around the world in three months," Ralph said.

"Actually," Phileas interrupted, "it's just eighty days."

"Phileas is right," John said. "The paper said it would only take eighty days now that the great railroad in India is complete." He opened up the paper and showed it to his friends. "See here—it maps the whole trip out."

Each man took his turn looking at the paper. Right there in black and white was a description of how someone could travel around the world in eighty days.

"Even so," Ralph said, "that doesn't account

for bad weather, accidents, or any number of things that could throw a man off track."

"That's all included," Phileas said.

"What about problems with the railroad or getting lost?" Ralph argued.

"That's included as well. The paper has it all worked out, every possible thing that could go wrong, every last delay. It takes a mere eighty days to travel right around the world," Phileas said. He put down his cards and said, "Two trumps! I've won this hand!"

Andrew gathered up the cards, shuffled them, and then dealt. He said, "Maybe you're right, Phileas, but I still don't believe it can be done."

"I know it can be done," Phileas replied.

Andrew smiled. "If that's the case, then how about a bet? I'd wager four thousand pounds that it's impossible to go around the world in just eighty days."

"It's very possible," Phileas insisted.

"Well, why don't *you* do it then?!" Andrew said.

"I'd like nothing better," Phileas replied. "I will show you myself that I can make it around the world in just eighty days."

"So you'll take my wager?" Andrew asked.

Phileas smiled and said, "Absolutely. And I've got twenty thousand pounds at the bank that I'm willing to risk as well."

"Come now," Samuel said. "Are you both being serious?"

"I am!" Andrew shouted.

"As am I!" Phileas said.

"Very well," Thomas said. "We're all here to witness that Phileas Fogg shall attempt to win his bet with Andrew Stuart by traveling around the world in eighty days."

"Correct!" Phileas said. "I will make a tour of the world in eighty days or less."

The five men said together: "Very good!"

"Very good!" Phileas said. "There's a train

leaving for Dover at eight forty-five tonight. I shall be on it."

"This very evening?" Andrew asked.

"This very evening," Phileas replied. He took a small calendar out of his pocket and looked at it carefully. "Today is Wednesday, October 2. I will be back in this room at eight forty-five p.m. on Saturday, December 21, or else my money belongs to you!"

The men signed a piece of paper sealing the wager, as gentlemen do. Phileas remained calm even though he had just bet half his fortune. He took a deep breath and said, "Let's have one last round of cards, gentlemen, before I head out."

CHAPTER 3

Phileas Fogg Shocks His New Butler

ᕔᕓ

Phileas Fogg left the Reform Club at exactly seven twenty-five. When he opened the door, he shouted for his new butler. "Passepartout!" he called out. "Passepartout!" he called again when he didn't get an answer.

"Passepartout!" Phileas shouted once more. Passepartout appeared at the bedroom door. "I've called you three times," Phileas said.

"But it's not yet midnight, sir," the butler replied.

"I know," Phileas said, "but we're leaving for Dover in ten minutes."

A puzzled grin spread over Passepartout's face. "Monsieur is leaving on a trip?"

"Yes," Phileas replied. "We are going on a trip around the world." He paused. "We must be back in eighty days." Passepartout opened his eyes wide. Then he raised his eyebrows and held up his hands in disbelief.

"A tour of the world?" he asked in shock.

"In eighty days," Phileas repeated. "We haven't a moment to spare."

"But that's not enough time to pack your trunk, sir," Passepartout said.

"We're not taking trunks. Just carpetbags with two shirts and three pairs of socks each. We'll have to buy anything else we need along the way."

Passepartout left the room feeling stunned. Carpetbags were so small—they barely had enough room for what one needed for an overnight trip. *Around the world*, he thought. *And in eighty days! Is the monsieur crazy?*

Passepartout had everything packed by eight o'clock. He carefully shut the door to his room and went downstairs to where Phileas was waiting. Phileas carried two travel guides under his arm—one for the railways and one for the boats. He put both books and his wallet into the carpetbag Passepartout held out for him.

"You haven't forgotten anything?" Phileas asked.

"Not a thing, sir," Passepartout said.

"My hat and cloak?" Phileas asked.

"Right here, sir." Passepartout handed them to him. Phileas took his hat and coat and handed his bag to his butler. "Now be careful with my bag," he said. "There's twenty thousand pounds in it!" Passepartout was so shocked that he nearly dropped the bag.

The two went outside and stepped into a waiting cab. It took them directly to the railroad station. Once inside, Phileas bought the tickets.

At twenty minutes before nine, Phileas and Passepartout found their seats in the first-class cabin. They had made it to the train with five minutes to spare. Passepartout held on tightly to the carpetbag with monsieur's money. He still couldn't quite believe what was happening. The train's whistle blew, and they were off!

CHAPTER 4

Introducing Detective Fix

～

The whirlwind trip had begun! In a mere four days of traveling, Passepartout and Phileas had already left Europe. They had traveled by train to Dover and then sailed to Paris from there. From Paris they took a train to Turin, Italy. Another train carried them through Italy to Brindisi, where they boarded a steamer called the *Mongolia*.

The *Mongolia* was due to arrive at the Suez Canal on Wednesday, October 9, at exactly eleven o'clock in the morning. It was one of the fastest steamers that the Peninsular and Oriental Company owned.

While the boat moved toward the Suez, two men walked up and down the canal. One was the British diplomat for the area. His name was Stephenson. The other was one of the detectives the Bank of England had sent around the world looking for the robber. His name was Fix.

Mr. Fix was a short man with small eyes and bushy eyebrows that twitched constantly. Despite his mouse-like appearance, he was a smart detective. It was his job to watch every single passenger that landed in Suez. He was to report anyone who looked like he might be the robber.

"So, Stephenson," Fix said for the twentieth time, "you say that this steamer is *always* on time?"

Mr. Stephenson sighed. "Yes, Mr. Fix. That is correct. If anything, the *Mongolia* sometimes gets here ahead of time."

"And it comes directly from Brindisi, Italy?" the detective asked.

"Again, that is correct. The ship collects the mail and then leaves at five o'clock on Saturday afternoon. The schedule is always the same. The *Mongolia* should be here at exactly eleven," Stephenson said. "Have patience, Mr. Fix. Anyway, I don't see how you're going to find the man you're looking for with the description you have of him. He could be anyone. There are many gentlemen who travel here from Italy."

"Ah!" Fix said quickly, "but one just knows, sir, when they're in the company of a bad man. One has a scent of them—a sixth sense that combines hearing, seeing, and smelling! That's how I can tell."

"Even if the man is a gentleman?" Stephenson asked.

"I shall sniff the man right out, even if he *is* a gentleman!" Fix said.

It was now half past ten. The wharf was getting busy. Sailors, merchants, shipbuilders, and porters all walked by. Detective Fix looked carefully at each person who passed him.

"The *Mongolia* still isn't here!" Fix said.

"The ship will be here on time," Stephenson repeated.

"How long does it stop at Suez?" Fix asked.

"For four hours. Just long enough to get a new supply of coal," Stephenson answered.

"And then the steamer travels directly to Bombay?"

"It stops in Aden for more coal, but then it goes on to Bombay," Stephenson said.

"Good," said Fix. "If the robber is on board, he'll probably get off here. He'll want to make his way to Asia, where he can't be caught, rather than India, which is part of the Queen's empire."

"Unless he stayed in England to hide," Stephenson replied.

"Not likely!" Fix said. "Not likely!"

Stephenson went back to his office and left Fix alone on the wharf. Fix paced back and forth on the docks, thinking. Soon a few sharp whistles blew. The *Mongolia* was here! The porters rushed onto the dock and a number of boats rowed out to meet the steamer. The *Mongolia* dropped her anchor in Suez at exactly eleven o'clock—just as Stephenson had said it would.

Fix stood back and watched everyone. After pushing his way through the crowd, one of the passengers came up to him. It was Passepartout.

"Excuse me, sir. Where might I find the British passport office?" He held out a passport that needed to be stamped.

The detective took the passport and asked, "Is this yours?"

"No, sir," Passepartout said. "It's the monsieur's—my boss's."

"Who is your boss?" Fix asked.

"Mr. Phileas Fogg, sir. He stayed on board," Passepartout replied.

"Well, he must go see the British diplomat in person to get his passport stamped," Fix said. "It's just over there—that house on the corner."

"Thank you, sir. He won't be happy about this at all!"

Passepartout pushed his way back through the crowds to tell Phileas that he had to visit the office himself. Fix, too, made his way to the corner house. He was curious about the gentleman who had sent his butler to get his passport stamped.

It must be him, Fix thought to himself. *The robber—he doesn't want to be seen!*

"I have found him!" Fix announced to Stephenson as he walked into the diplomat's office. "He's on board the *Mongolia*, just as I suspected. He's headed here to get his passport stamped. I just ran into his butler, who said that his boss refuses to leave the boat. I told the servant that the man must come in person! We've got him now!"

"He might not come, you know," Stephenson said.

"If he does, you must not stamp his passport," Fix told him.

"But I have no choice if the passport is real," Stephenson said.

"I want to keep this man here until I can get a warrant for his arrest," Fix said.

"But I cannot—" A knock at the door stopped the diplomat mid-sentence. Passepartout and Phileas entered the room. Fix stood in the corner and watched as Phileas held out his passport.

"Kind sir, would you please stamp my passport?" Phileas asked.

Stephenson took it from him and looked at it closely. "You know that you don't need to get your passport stamped," Stephenson said. He was about to hand the passport back to Phileas.

"I know, but I wish to prove I was here."

Stephenson stamped and dated the passport. Phileas paid the fee, bowed slightly, and then left.

"Well?" Fix said.

"He looks and acts like a perfectly honest man," Stephenson said.

"But do you not think he looks just like the robber?" Fix asked.

"I suppose, but it was a very general description, Fix," Stephenson said.

"It's him! I know it's him!" Fix said.

❧

Fix followed Phileas and Passepartout back down to the dock. Phileas went back on board the

Mongolia. He wanted to make some notes about how the trip was going. Passepartout stayed on the wharf and looked around.

Fix walked up to him and said, "Having a look around?"

"We travel so fast that I like to see what I can," Passepartout replied. "So this is Egypt?"

"Indeed it is."

"In Africa?" he asked.

"Yes," Fix answered.

"Africa!" Passepartout exclaimed. "To think, I had never been farther than Paris before. That is my home town. But we passed through there so quickly that all I got to see this time was the trip between the Northern and the Lyon stations."

"You're in a hurry, then?" Fix asked. He was trying not to ask too many questions.

"I am not, but monsieur is. He's making a tour of the world," Passepartout answered.

"A tour of the world!" Fix said.

"Yes, and in eighty days," Passepartout said. "He says it's a bet, but between the two of us, I'm not sure about that. There must be something else going on."

"Indeed!" Fix added.

"The monsieur is a rich man. He's carrying a large amount of new bank notes with him and he'll do anything to win."

"Indeed!" Fix said again. "Have you known Mr. Fogg a long time?"

"No. I just started working for him the day we left!" Passepartout said. "I must be on my way. I have to buy some new shirts for the monsieur before going back on board. We're on our way to Bombay next!"

The facts were almost too much for Fix to handle. There was the quick departure from London and the large sum of money that Phileas Fogg carried with him. There was also the fact that Phileas needed to reach faraway countries in

a hurry. Not to mention that he fit the description of the robber—he was a gentleman. Fix ran off to the diplomat's office to send a telegram to London.

Fix looked at the telegram closely before he gave it to the clerk. It read:

SUEZ TO LONDON

TO: ROWAN, POLICE CHIEF, SCOTLAND YARD

FROM: DETECTIVE FIX

I'VE FOUND THE BANK ROBBER. PHILEAS FOGG.

SEND ARREST WARRANT TO BOMBAY. I WILL MEET

HIM THERE.

CHAPTER 5

Phileas Fogg Travels Across the Red Sea and the Indian Ocean

༄

The *Mongolia* left Suez on schedule—at exactly three p.m. local time—and started off on its journey to Aden. Phileas Fogg didn't care for sight-seeing, so he spent little time on deck. Instead he passed his time much as he did at the Reform Club—he ate his meals and played cards.

Unlike his boss, Passepartout truly enjoyed the scenery. He took every chance he could get to stand on deck and watch what passed by.

One day when he was out and about, he came

across Detective Fix. "Oh," Passepartout said, "you are the kind gentleman I met in Suez!"

"And you are the butler to that strange Englishman!" Fix said.

"That's correct, Monsieur—"

"Fix."

"Fix," Passepartout repeated. "I'm happy to see you on board. Where are you going?"

"To Bombay."

"Why, that's exactly where we're going! Have you been to India before?" Passepartout asked.

Fix told him that he had indeed been to India. To disguise his true identity as a London detective, he told Passepartout that he was an agent for the Peninsular and Oriental Company. This was the same company that owned the *Mongolia*. The two men became fast friends and quickly started taking daily walks around the deck together. As they walked, they chatted about what life must be like in India.

Fix tried to get Passepartout to tell him more about Phileas Fogg and his curious trip around the world. Passepartout always answered honestly, but he didn't know much. What little he could share was rarely of any interest to Detective Fix.

Meanwhile, the *Mongolia* pushed onward. They passed Mocha, drove through the Straight of Bab-el Mandeb, and then stopped at Aden for more coal. They were still sixteen hundred miles away from Bombay.

Fogg once again went on shore to have his passport stamped. He returned to the ship while Passepartout had a look around. By six o'clock, they were back on the ocean. The journey from Aden to Bombay was to take just seven short days. The Indian Ocean was smooth and calm. In fact, the *Mongolia* made excellent time. It arrived two days early!

When they reached the port, Phileas calmly

entered the two-day gain in his diary. He also noted the time and the number of miles they had traveled.

⌒

After saying good-bye to his card partners on board the *Mongolia*, Phileas gave Passepartout some errands to run and set off in search of the passport office. They already had their tickets for the great railway that crossed India from Bombay to Calcutta. It was set to leave for Calcutta at exactly eight o'clock that evening. Phileas wanted Passepartout to make sure he was back by then.

With his stamped passport in hand, Phileas set off for the railway station to have his dinner. As for the wonders of Bombay, he didn't truly care to see them.

While Phileas tried to eat an awful meal of strange meat, Fix went off in search of the Bombay police station. He told them he was a detective from London on the trail of a robber. He wanted to know if his warrant had arrived—it had not. Fix tried to convince the police to write a new one, but they refused. They said it was a matter for the London police. Fix did not argue with them. He knew that Phileas Fogg wouldn't be staying in Bombay for very long anyway. He would have to find another way to catch him.

Meanwhile, Passepartout set off on his errands right away. He had begun to believe that they were indeed on a race around the world. Having bought the new shirts and socks that Phileas had asked for, he took his time exploring Bombay's busy streets and crowded market squares. People wore dresses of all different designs! There were pointed caps and turbans, square bonnets, and long robes. Everyone looked so different!

During his walk, Passepartout found himself in the middle of a parade. Girls in pretty costumes danced while shaking noisy tambourines. When the show had passed, Passepartout found himself drawn to a temple. What he didn't know was that foreigners were forbidden from entering these temples. It was against the law for him to go in!

Passepartout had barely stepped inside when all of the sudden he was on the floor! Three very angry priests were hitting him and yelling in a strange language. Then they pulled off his shoes! Passepartout jumped to his feet, pushed away two of his attackers, and ran out the door as fast as he could.

By the time he made it to the railway station, it was five minutes to eight. He had lost his package of new socks and shirts in the scuffle. Passepartout tried to explain what had happened, but Phileas was not happy with him.

"I hope this won't happen again," he said as they boarded the train. Passepartout hung his head in shame and promised that it wouldn't. The last thing he wanted was to make the monsieur unhappy with him.

Fix was two steps behind them. He was about to board the train when suddenly he changed his mind. He had heard every word and knew exactly what had happened to Passepartout. "A crime has been committed on Indian soil," he whispered to himself. He thought about the error Passepartout had made by entering the temple. "That's how I'll catch them!"

Fix sent a telegram to Calcutta, telling the police there to expect Mr. Fogg and Passepartout, and explaining what had happened in the temple. Then he booked himself on the next train, taking every step to make sure he got to Calcutta before them.

CHAPTER 6

Phileas Fogg Rides an Elephant!

༄

The whistle blew and the train set off right on time. Only one other person was sitting in the cabin with Passepartout and Phileas. His name was Sir Francis Cromarty. A tall, fair man of fifty, Sir Francis was on his way to join his British troops stationed at Benares, another major city in India.

Phileas and Sir Francis had met on board the *Mongolia*, where they had played cards together. Sir Francis, a general in the British army, thought Phileas was quite mad to attempt to travel the world in such a short time. In fact, he thought Phileas was a strange fellow indeed.

They had been traveling for many hours when Sir Francis said, "Some years ago, Phileas, you would have gotten stuck here. It would have lost you your bet."

"How so?" Phileas asked.

"The railway used to stop at the base of these mountains. The passengers had to ride through on ponies to get to the other side."

"Ah," Phileas said, "well, I would have planned for that. It would have been fine."

While the two men spoke, Passepartout slept quietly wrapped up in a blanket. Finally the men stopped talking and rode in silence. The train drove on through the night. By morning, it had left the mountains behind.

The first stop they made after leaving Bombay was Burhampoor. While the train stopped for supplies and coal, Passepartout bought himself some new shoes. After all, he had left his behind in the scuffle at the temple. The new shoes were Indian slippers decorated with false pearls. Passepartout had never owned anything so lovely.

Once they were back on their way, Passepartout sat back down and looked out the window. He was amazed to be in India of all places. In fact, he was coming around to the idea of the whirlwind trip. He was even starting to enjoy himself.

Then the train stopped. "All passengers will get out here!" the conductor shouted.

Phileas looked over to Sir Francis, but he didn't know why they were stopping either. Outside was a small village surrounded by a forest of palm trees. Passepartout rushed off the train to see what was going on.

"Monsieur!" he said when he got back, "there's no more railroad!"

"What do you mean?" Sir Francis asked.

"I mean to say the train can go no farther," Passepartout answered.

The general stepped out, followed by Phileas Fogg. They both went to talk to the conductor.

"What's going on?" Sir Francis asked.

"The railroad's not finished. There are still fifty miles to build. You'll need to find your own way from here."

With that, the conductor left the three men. None of them knew quite what to do next.

The London papers had all been wrong—the great railway across India was *almost* finished.

"Surely this will be a problem. You'll never make your connection in Calcutta now," Sir Francis said.

"On the contrary," Phileas said, "I have a few

days to spare. Today is only October twenty-second. The steamer doesn't leave for Hong Kong until the twenty-fifth. We'll make it to Calcutta yet.

"We'll have to go by foot," Phileas decided. Passepartout looked down at his new shoes. They would not make a fifty-mile walk. He looked around him for a minute and then said, "Monsieur, I think I might have found another way!"

"What's that, Passepartout?" Phileas said.

"An elephant!" He pointed to a small hut a few yards from the station. Indeed, there was an elephant standing there. The three men walked over to the hut and knocked on the door. An Indian man came outside and showed them Kiouni, for that was the elephant's name.

Phileas tried to hire the elephant to take them to Allahabad, where the train tracks started again, but her owner said no. He offered more money,

but the answer was still no. After many minutes of this back-and-forth, Phileas offered a price of six hundred pounds. Still no! Then he tried to buy Kiouni for one thousand pounds. Still no! It took an offer of two thousand pounds for the man to agree.

"Two thousand pounds!" Passepartout said, "for an elephant!" He was amazed that his boss was willing to spend so much money!

But now the men had to find a guide. In town they found a nice young man named Ali. They hired him right away. They bought supplies and were soon ready to go. Phileas and Sir Francis sat in seats on either side of the elephant. These were called *howdahs*. Passepartout sat in between the two men. He was right on Kiouni's back. The guide sat on the elephant's neck. They set off from the village at nine o'clock and started marching through the forest of palm trees around them.

CHAPTER 7

Phileas Fogg, Passepartout, and Sir Francis Have an Adventure

ᕙ

Nestled up to their necks in the *howdahs*, Sir Francis and Phileas were tossed about by the elephant as she ran through the forest. Ali had told them that they could save a lot of time by taking a shortcut, and so there they were, but it was much rougher than the normal road. Passepartout bounced around on the elephant's back. It may have hurt, but Passepartout was enjoying himself. He felt like a clown on a vault.

The men rode through a thick forest and then through dry fields. They saw some animals—mainly monkeys—that Passepartout quite liked. The passengers were a bit scared of traveling through this rough territory on the way to Allahabad. They knew there were gangs of bandits who ruled the lands there and no one wanted any trouble.

Although he loved being atop an elephant, Passepartout wondered what the monsieur was going to do with Kiouni once they arrived at Allahabad. He thought about this for a long while as they moved swiftly along.

By that evening, the men had gone half the distance to the other railway station. It was a cold night. They stopped at a run-down hut, where their guide lit a nice warm fire. Kiouni slept outside, leaning up against a large tree. Soon the snores of the travelers floated through the air.

By six o'clock the next morning, they were on the way again. Ali wanted to get them to the railway station that evening. This meant that Phileas would only lose a small bit of the time he had gained since starting his trip. With only twelve miles to go, the men stopped under a banana tree and had a snack.

After the break, Ali led Kiouni back into the forest. They had avoided all signs of the bandits so far and he wanted to keep it that way.

Suddenly Kiouni stopped.

"What's the matter?" Sir Francis asked. He stuck his head out of his *howdah*. The men heard loud voices coming through the woods.

"Quickly," Ali said. "We must hide."

He led Kiouni off the trail so the people who were coming wouldn't see them. The clanging of instruments and loud voices crept closer and closer. A group of men dressed in costumes pulled a cart with an ugly statue on it.

Sir Francis whispered, "Do you think they've seen us?" Ali made a motion with his hand for him to be quiet.

Some of the men danced around the statue. Many of them were wearing long robes. Another group pulled a woman behind them. She fell down with almost every step she took. She was young, pretty, and wore gems on her hands, feet, neck, arms, and legs. The guards who followed her carried giant sabers and very sharp swords.

"I think they mean to harm that poor girl," Sir Francis whispered.

"I think you're right," Phileas said. "She must be a princess. Look at the way she is dressed. I have twelve hours to spare—we must save her!"

"Agreed!" Sir Francis said.

"Agreed!" Passepartout added.

"If they catch you, they will surely torture you," Ali said. "But you have my help as well. The girl they have captured is the daughter of a wealthy merchant in Bombay. Her name is Aouda. She is very famous."

"That makes sense. They must have captured her for the ransom her family would pay to get her back!" Phileas said. "Let's think of a plan. It might be best to wait for the cover of darkness."

Everyone nodded. "We should move our camp closer to them. That way we can see what they're doing," Sir Francis added.

They tied up Kiouni and made their way closer to the camp. A large fire burned and they heard a great commotion. The men planned to cut open the wall of the hut where the girl was being kept and steal her away. They waited until it was dark and the guards had fallen asleep. Then Passepartout and Ali slipped away and started breaking down the wall. Phileas and Sir Francis watched from behind a nearby tree.

"Oh, no!" Phileas whispered. "The guard has woken up! We've got to do something before he finds Passepartout."

The two men slowly snuck up behind the guard and hit him on the head. They didn't want to hurt him too badly. They just wanted to make sure he stayed asleep. Sir Francis and Phileas joined Passepartout and Ali digging away at the wall. Finally they were through!

The poor girl lay on the bed. She looked half-dead. Passepartout carefully picked her up. "Hurry!" Phileas said, "we've got to get out of here right away!"

The men crept through the small hole in the wall and quickly ran back to Kiouni. But they had been seen! The bandits chased them through the woods. Arrows whizzed by their heads. Ali ran ahead, as fast as he could. He would need to help everyone onto the elephant. They climbed on and raced away with Kiouni thundering through the forest.

"We did it!" Sir Francis shouted. "We did it! Well done everyone! Well done!"

Phileas safely tucked Aouda away in one of the *howdahs*. She was still sleeping soundly. She hadn't even woken up once! Then he joined Passepartout on top of the elephant, while Sir Francis took the other *howdah*.

CHAPTER 8

The Trip Down the Ganges

~

The party made rapid progress toward Allahabad. They moved so quickly, in fact, that they reached the train station by mid-morning.

Once they arrived in Allahabad, Phileas asked Passepartout to run some errands. Passepartout was happy to do so. Besides, he was eager to explore the city.

By the time Passepartout returned, it was time to say good-bye to Ali. Phileas paid him and said, "Ali, you have been such a great help to us— would you like to keep Kiouni?"

"Sir! Are you sure? She is worth a fortune," Ali replied. "That is so kind of you! I can't believe it!"

"It is a well deserved gift," Phileas said.

Passepartout said, "Oh, I am so glad you are going to take her, Ali. Kiouni will be a brave and faithful friend."

He patted the elephant's trunk. Kiouni, in turn, picked up Passepartout and lifted him high into the air. The butler laughed and patted the elephant on the head. Kiouni gently placed him back down on the ground.

A whistle blew. It was time to board the train. Sir Francis carried Aouda and carefully set her down in the cabin. Soon they were speeding along toward Benares. A few hours later, Aouda woke up. She was startled and scared. She was also surprised to be on a speeding train and not trapped in a hut with bandits all around.

"Where am I?" she asked.

"You are safe now, dear girl," Phileas replied.

"We have saved you from those awful men and are taking you to Benares with us. My name is Phileas Fogg. This is my butler, Passepartout, and our friend Sir Francis."

She thanked them all for their help in saving her life and said she would never be able to repay them for everything they had done.

"Nonsense. It was our pleasure," Phileas said.

"My family has all been killed by the bandits. They would have killed me, too, if you hadn't saved me."

"That means your life will always be in danger if you stay here. Would you like us to take you to Hong Kong? That is where we are headed next."

"That would be appreciated," Aouda said quietly. "Thank you again for all your kindness."

When the train reached Benares, the travelers said good-bye to Sir Francis. He wished them all success and said that he hoped to see them again soon.

CHAPTER 9

Phileas Fogg Spends a Lot of Money

The train entered the station in Calcutta and the passengers climbed off. Phileas wanted to get going right away so they could board the Hong Kong steamer in plenty of time. They had a few hours before it was due to leave. Phileas wanted to make sure Aouda was comfortable and had everything she needed. Of course, that meant that Passepartout would have to run some errands.

A policeman stopped Phileas just after he had helped Aouda down from the train. "Are you Mr. Phileas Fogg?" he asked.

"I am," Phileas replied.

"And this man is your butler?" He pointed to Passepartout.

"He is."

"Then both of you need to come with me." The policeman walked toward a carriage and opened the door for them. Not wanting to leave Aouda behind, Phileas told her to come with them.

After a quiet twenty-minute journey, they arrived at a small house. The policeman opened up the carriage door. As he let them out, he said, "Follow me."

He led the three of them into a small room with bars on the windows. "You'll stand before Judge Obadiah at precisely eight-thirty."

"We are prisoners?" Phileas exclaimed. "Nonsense! There must be some mistake." He turned to Aouda and Passepartout. "Not to worry, we shall be on board the steamer by noon."

The door opened and the policeman came back. He brought them into the courtroom.

Judge Obadiah, a fat, round man, came in.

"The first case!" The judge called.

"Phileas Fogg!" the judge's clerk shouted.

"Present," Phileas said.

Three men came into the courtroom. At first Phileas and Passepartout thought they were members of the gang trying to get Aouda back. But then one of them produced Passepartout's shoes!

"Mr. Passepartout, you are charged with illegally entering a temple. These shoes are the proof that you were indeed there," the judge said.

"My shoes!" Passepartout said loudly.

"So you *do* admit you were there?"

Passepartout nodded slowly.

"Good. You will be fined one hundred and fifty pounds and will need to spend one week in jail."

Phileas spoke up. "I shall pay his bail. Then he won't need to stay in jail. What's the cost?"

The judge looked at him. "It's rather steep, sir. Two thousand pounds."

Phileas took a roll of bills out of his carpetbag and paid the bail.

Detective Fix stood at the back of the courtroom watching everything. He thought he had found a sure-fire way of keeping Phileas in India until he could get the proper arrest warrant. But now that Passepartout had bail, it looked like Phileas was going to get away again! He had never imagined  the robber would be so free with his money.

"Good," said the judge. "This money will be returned to you once Passepartout has completed his time in jail. If he doesn't return, we shall keep the money."

Phileas nodded. "That's fine, sir." He turned to Passepartout and Aouda, and said, "Let's go!" Passepartout grabbed his shoes on the way out. "We need to be on our way to the wharf right now!"

With a heavy heart, Passepartout followed his monsieur. He did not enjoy having his boss spend money on mistakes that he had made. He glanced up to see Fix standing off in the corner looking very angry indeed. For a second, Passepartout wondered what he was doing there, but he was in too much of a hurry to give the matter much thought.

CHAPTER 10

The Voyage from India to Hong Kong

The three travelers boarded the *Rangoon* just in time. The steamer was just about to set off for Hong Kong. During the first few days of the trip, Aouda spent much of her time getting to know Phileas and Passepartout. She told them her life story. Her father had been a very wealthy merchant who dealt in cotton. They had lived a wonderful life until he ran into trouble with the bandits. Then she told them about her cousin, Jeejah Jeejeebhoy, who lived in Hong Kong.

As on the *Mongolia*, Passepartout often spent

his afternoons walking around on deck. One day as he strolled along, he was shocked to see Mr. Fix!

"Why, sir!" Passepartout said, "what on Earth are you doing here? I left you in Bombay, saw you briefly in Calcutta, and now here you are on the way to Hong Kong. Are you making a tour of the world, too?"

"No, no. I shall be stopping in Hong Kong," Fix said.

Indeed, Fix had sent another telegram to London asking for the arrest warrant to follow him there. It was his last chance to catch Phileas Fogg, the bank robber. Once he left Hong Kong and entered America, he would no longer be on British soil. That meant Fix would no longer be able to arrest him. Fix was frustrated with his progress so far. He was tired of chasing Phileas around the world.

"How is it that I haven't seen you since we left Calcutta?" Passepartout asked.

"Oh, I've been seasick," Fix said. "How is Mr. Fogg?"

"Quite well. And he's not a day behind time! We now have a young woman traveling with us, too!"

Fix pretended to look surprised. Passepartout told him the story of how they had rescued Aouda from the bandits in India.

"Will Aouda be traveling back to Europe with you?" Fix asked.

"Oh no, she's going to stay with her cousin in Hong Kong. She'll be safe there."

As they had done just about every afternoon on board the *Mongolia*, the two shared a drink of lemonade and a walk around the deck.

As the days passed, Passepartout began to think it was quite strange that he should keep running into Mr. Fix. At once, Passepartout had a chilling thought. *He must be following us!*

That's it! Passepartout thought. *He must be a spy*

sent from the Reform Club. And my monsieur is such an honest man—that's just terrible! He decided not to tell Phileas. He didn't want him to think poorly of his friends from the club, so he kept it to himself. He also didn't want Mr. Fix to realize that he knew. That might cause problems between Phileas Fogg and the Reform Club, and the last thing Passepartout wanted to do was cause the monsieur more trouble!

The *Rangoon* landed in Singapore a half-day before schedule. As usual, Phileas noted this in his journal. He also sent Passepartout off on his usual errands. Aouda wanted to see a bit of the island, so she and Phileas took a carriage ride. They rode through the country smelling clove and nutmeg trees. They saw full, green ferns, and row upon row of palm trees.

They toured the city as well, passing by interesting houses with charming gardens. By late morning they were back on board the *Rangoon*, ready to set sail again. Passepartout had finished his errands and bought some fresh fruit, which he shared with Aouda once she was back on board. All three bid good-bye to Singapore as the ship moved out of the harbor and set its course for Hong Kong.

⁓

The first few days of the journey were uneventful. They had good weather and fair winds. About halfway through the twelve-day trip, the weather turned. The sea started to roll heavily as a storm brewed. The ship fell behind schedule. This upset Passepartout, but Phileas Fogg remained calm.

He spent his days with Aouda and his nights making notes.

One day Fix found Passepartout pacing around the top deck of the ship.

"You're in a great hurry today!" he said.

"A great hurry," Passepartout said. "The

weather is slowing us down and this ship is not going fast enough."

"So you now believe in this around the world tour?" Fix asked.

"Absolutely, Mr. Fix. Don't you believe in it?" Passepartout winked at him and then walked away.

The wink confused Fix. Did it mean that Passepartout knew he was a detective? Had he been found out? The next day the two men met up once again.

"Ah," Passepartout said, "shall we be seeing you on the way to America, too, Mr. Fix?" He winked again.

"Um, oh, uh," Fix stuttered, "I don't know."

"It's odd. You were only going as far as Bombay, but then you were in Calcutta. And now you're going to Hong Kong."

Passepartout slapped Fix on the back as he walked away. Fix went back to his cabin, lost in thought. The butler must have found out the truth.

There's only one thing I can do, he thought to himself. *I must tell Passepartout everything.*

⌒

The wind blew harder each day. The boat rolled on the giant waves. The steamer was forced to sail very slowly. Now they would be a full day late arriving in Hong Kong. Phileas was still calm, even though this delay meant he would surely lose his bet. He had used up all of his extra time in India when they had to travel by elephant, and was hoping to have made up some time. Aouda was surprised that he was not at all worried about the fact they would now miss the boat from Hong Kong to Japan.

Of course, Fix was happy about the delay. It meant that his warrant had even more time to arrive. And then there was Passepartout. The poor man paced up and down and back and forth. He was so worried.

When the ship finally docked in Hong Kong, the three travelers left the *Rangoon* and went to find out about the steamer to Yokohama. Phileas asked at the passport office whether or not they had missed it.

"Why, no," said the officer who stamped his passport. "They had a problem with one of the boilers. It is delayed until high tide tomorrow morning."

"Ah," said Phileas without a hint of emotion. "What is the steamer called?"

"The *Carnatic*," the officer said. "The ticket office is just down the street."

Passepartout grabbed the man's hand. He pumped it up and down and said energetically, "Thank you! Thank you! You are the best of all good fellows!"

Luck was on their side! If the boat had not had

to stop for repairs, they would have had to wait a week before traveling on to Japan. Phileas booked rooms for them at the Club Hotel. They would stay there until they boarded the steamer tomorrow. It was set to leave at five o'clock the next morning. With that taken care of, he left Aouda with Passepartout to keep her company and set off to find her cousin Jeejah Jeejeebhoy.

While in the market, Phileas came across a merchant who knew Jeejah Jeejeebhoy. The merchant told him that Mr. Jeejeebhoy had left Hong Kong two years ago and moved to Holland.

When Phileas got back to the hotel, he sat down with Aouda and told her that her cousin had moved away.

At first she said nothing. She just sat there thinking. Then, in her sweet, soft voice she said, "What should I do, Phileas?"

"It is very simple," he said. "You must go on to Europe."

"But I cannot be in your way——"

"Nonsense, you're not in the way at all. It is our pleasure to have you along on our trip," Phileas said. "Passepartout!"

"Monsieur?"

"Please book three cabins on the *Carnatic*. We're all going to Japan. From there we'll go on to America."

Passepartout was very happy that Aouda would still be traveling with them. He skipped happily out of the room to run his errand.

CHAPTER 11

Passepartout Takes Too Great an Interest in Phileas Fogg, and What Comes of It

⌒

Passepartout walked around Hong Kong with his hands in his pockets. The port had ships from all around the world: England, France, the Americas, Holland, Japan, and China. When he reached the dock where he was to book the cabins on the *Carnatic*, he saw Fix there. He was not surprised.

The detective himself did not look happy. His warrant still had not arrived.

"Well, well, Fix," Passepartout said, "have you decided to join us on our journey to America?"

"Yes," Fix said through gritted teeth.

"Good!" Passepartout said. "I knew you would end up with us! Come, let's book our cabins."

The men went into the steamer office, where the clerk told them that the ship was now fixed. It would be leaving that evening instead of tomorrow morning.

"Wonderful!" Passepartout said. "I'll go tell the monsieur. He'll be very pleased."

Fix decided that now was the right time to tell Passepartout everything. He knew it was the only way to keep Phileas Fogg in Hong Kong until the warrant arrived. He asked the butler if he wanted to share a meal with him, and the two went into a small restaurant near the wharf.

Once inside, the men found themselves in a large room filled with comfortable chairs and lots of cushions. They chatted for a while over dinner. When Passepartout finished his meal, he got up to leave. "Wait," Fix said. "I have something else I want to talk to you about."

"It shall have to wait. I must tell monsieur about the steamer leaving early."

"Stay! What I have to say concerns Mr. Fogg." Fix placed his hand on Passepartout's arm and said quietly, "You've guessed who I am?"

Passepartout smiled. "I have indeed."

"Then you must know that my job involves a lot of money," Fix said. "I'm willing to give you some if you'll keep Mr. Fogg in Hong Kong. Don't tell him about the ship."

"Not tell him! That's going too far, sir. I thought the members of the Reform Club were honest men."

Fix looked at Passepartout strangely for a moment. "Who do you think I am?"

"Why, you're a spy sent to follow us and make sure that Phileas makes an honest trip around the world. Maybe you've also been sent to interfere, but I won't let that happen," Passepartout said. "I haven't said anything to the monsieur yet, though."

"So he knows nothing?" Fix said. "Oh, just a moment. I'll get us some cocoa."

Fix got up and left the table. On his way to ask for the cocoa, he stopped to speak to a man in a dark corner of the room. Fix had asked this man to accompany him to the restaurant. He was an associate of the police department in Hong Kong. He knew he had to do something. Phileas could not leave Hong Kong.

Fix returned to the table with two mugs of cocoa. "Passepartout," Fix began, "I am afraid you are mistaken. I am not a member of the Reform Club. I am a detective from London. Your master is a robber. He has stolen a great deal of money from the Bank of England and I've been sent to get it back. You must help me keep him in Hong Kong until I can arrest him."

Passepartout's mouth dropped wide open. "A

robber!" he said. "He is not a robber! He is the most honorable of all men!"

Fix told Passepartout that the description of the robber perfectly matched Phileas Fogg. The robber was a gentleman, just like Phileas Fogg. The robber had access to a lot of money, just like Phileas. He was of the right height and build, too—everything added up.

Fix reminded the butler how little he knew about his boss. After all, he had only started working for him on the day they left. "Now, will you help me keep him in Hong Kong?" Fix asked again.

"I refuse. The monsieur is a fine gentleman. He did not commit this crime. I don't believe you. I am leaving now."

"I wish you would change your mind." As Passepartout got up to leave, Fix nodded to the man from the back corner. Suddenly the man crept up behind Passepartout and knocked him on the head. Passepartout fell down to the ground! The man nodded to Fix before running out the door so he wouldn't be seen.

"At last!" Fix said to himself as he picked up the butler and put him on a cushioned chair. "Mr. Fogg will not know that the steamer is leaving early. He'll be forced to stay in Hong Kong for another week!"

With that, Fix left poor Passepartout unconscious in the restaurant.

∽

Phileas Fogg and Aouda were walking around Hong Kong buying supplies for the long voyage ahead of them. Neither one knew that the *Carnatic* would be leaving that evening. They spent the day shopping, had dinner, and then went back to their rooms to go to bed.

They didn't notice until the next morning that Passepartout was missing. Phileas and Aouda had gone to the wharf by themselves. They were hoping to meet the butler there, but when they arrived, they found Fix instead.

"Were you not a passenger on the *Rangoon*? I am a friend of your butler's," Fix said. "I was hoping to find him here."

"I was aboard the *Rangoon*. We are both looking for Passepartout. He did not return to the hotel last night," Phileas replied.

"That's strange, indeed!" Fix said.

"It is," Aouda agreed. "Do you think he's already on board the *Carnatic*?"

"Oh," Fix said, "I'm afraid I have some bad news. The *Carnatic* was fixed yesterday and left early. You've missed the boat. It'll be a week before another steamer leaves for Yokohama."

Phileas looked first at Fix and then around the harbor. He said quietly, "Well, we'll just have to take another boat then. Mr. Fix, would you please stay with Miss Aouda for a moment?"

Fix nodded slowly and then watched as Phileas quickly walked away. His heart sunk. *Another boat,* he thought. *He can't find another boat!*

A moment stretched to a minute, which stretched to an hour. Another hour passed before Phileas finally returned. "I've done it!" he said to them both. "I've found a boat that will take us to Shanghai. From there we can catch the *Carnatic* and go on to San Francisco!"

He turned to Fix. "I'm sure there is room if you would like to join us."

Putting on a false smile, Fix said, "Thank you, sir."

"Very well," Phileas said. "We leave in a half-hour."

"But Passepartout," Aouda said. "What's become of him? We need to find him."

"We'll do everything we can before we go, Aouda," Phileas said.

Fix rushed off to pack his things so he could

leave with them. Meanwhile, Phileas and Aouda went to the police station to try to find Passepartout. They left a sum of money with the police so they could search for Passepartout.

The boat Phileas had hired was called the *Tankadere*. Its captain was John Bunsby and it had a crew of four hearty sailors. When Aouda and Phileas went on board, they were surprised to find Fix already there.

"I'm sorry the cabins are so small," Phileas said, "but at least we don't have to wait another week to carry on!"

Fix bowed but didn't say anything. He thought, *he is a gentleman, I'll give him that.*

❦

It was now early November. The travelers had been away for over thirty-six days. Almost half the days they had were gone. The China Seas were rough and the wind was strong. The

Tankadere moved quickly. Captain Bunsby knew he had a solid ship and did everything possible to make it go as fast as it could.

Phileas Fogg stood on deck and looked out at the ever-growing waves. The boat rocked back and forth, but he never fell over. He had very strong sea legs. Great white sails flapped overhead. Aouda sat in a chair holding on for dear life.

Fix hid away in the cabin. He was upset that he had to follow Phileas all the way to America, but he had made a promise to himself that he wouldn't give up. He would do his duty to make sure he caught the robber. Despite how well he was being treated on board the *Tankadere,* Fix had to keep his mind on his task. It didn't matter that Phileas acted like the perfect gentleman— he was a criminal and it was Fix's job to catch him. Still, he was unhappy about the fact that Phileas had refused to take any of his money—either for food or for the boat trip. When Fix asked,

Phileas had flat out said they wouldn't speak of it. He said the journey was a part of his "general expense."

Well, Fix thought, *he does have the money, being a bank robber and all!*

The ship traveled over one hundred miles the first day. Phileas was happy about its progress. The captain was in great spirits. He felt sure they would reach Shanghai in time for Phileas to catch the *Carnatic.*

But on day three, everything changed. Dawn brought with it a dark and gloomy sky.

The captain stood on deck beside Phileas. The two men looked at the great clouds forming behind the boat.

"Sir," Captain Bunsby said, "I think we're in for quite a squall."

"I think so, too," Phileas said. "But the wind is blowing in the right direction to help us move forward."

The captain looked at his passenger. "So you wish for us to continue on this course?"

"Absolutely!" Phileas said.

The captain took a good look at Phileas Fogg and calmly noted that he was, in fact, serious.

❧

The boat rolled and shook. It kept its course for Shanghai even though it might have been safer to slow the boat down and stop at an earlier port. Day turned to night and then night back to day as the storm raged around them. There was not another boat in sight. The Tankadere was alone on the seas.

By noon on the second day, the storm finally slowed. They had but six hours to reach their destination or risk missing the steamer. All of a sudden, the wind died completely! How the skilled hands of Bunsby and his crew kept the boat moving was a complete mystery to Phileas and his companions. But move on they did.

They were a mere three miles from Shanghai when Phileas saw a long black funnel of steam ahead. It was the *Carnatic* leaving for Yokohama, where it would stop before heading to San Francisco!

"Signal her!" Phileas Fogg said.

A small brass cannon sat on deck of the *Tankadere*. It was supposed to be used for distress calls. The sailors loaded it up and lit the back.

"Fire!" Phileas shouted. The booming of the little cannon echoed in the air. The cannon caught the attention of the steamer, which in turn changed course to meet the *Tankadere*. Phileas Fogg and Aouda were able to board the *Carnatic*, and were back on the right course! Fix could not believe their luck.

CHAPTER 12

Passepartout Travels on Alone, and Grows a Very Long Nose

❧

The *Carnatic* left Hong Kong right on time, but with two empty rooms—ones that should have held Phileas Fogg and Aouda. The next day, a bleary-eyed passenger with wild and crazy hair stumbled out of his cabin and made his way up on deck. It was Passepartout!

Three hours after Fix had left him in that awful restaurant, he had woken up still dizzy from the knock to his head. He called out, "The *Carnatic*! The *Carnatic*!" as if he knew where he had to be. Barely able to stand, he pulled himself up and stumbled along to the ship. He fell on the deck just as it was leaving.

Two members of the crew had felt sorry for him and carried him to his cabin. When Passepartout woke up, it was the middle of the next day.

What will Mr. Fogg say when he sees me this way? he worried. *What in the world happened to me? At least I have made the boat.*

Passepartout got up and started to explore the ship. But he didn't see anyone who looked like either Phileas Fogg or Aouda. He went into the dining room to see if he could find either of them, but they were not there.

Finally Passepartout asked a ship's mate if he knew where he could find Phileas Fogg.

"There's no one by that name on board, sir," the mate replied.

"Am I on the *Carnatic*?" Passepartout asked.

"Yes."

"On the way to Yokohama?"

"Yes."

Passepartout fell into a seat as if struck by lightning. It was all coming back to him now! The monsieur must have missed the boat. Now Passepartout was on his way to Japan without a penny in his pocket. The trip was to take five or six days, so at least Passepartout had some time to figure out what to do.

When the boat docked in Yokohama, Passepartout stepped slowly off the ship and onto shore. He had nothing but fate to guide him as he walked the streets of the Japanese city. First he explored the European section of town. There he found many merchants selling their goods. Next he visited the French and the English consulates to see if they had heard any word from Phileas Fogg. With no luck there, he continued to explore the city.

What shall I do for food? he asked himself as he walked through the crowded streets. He looked into the windows of rich and curious shops. He saw teahouses and wished he had the money to sit down in one. Passepartout stayed hungry for much of that first day and night as he strolled around the city. He walked and walked. He never rested—not even when it turned to night.

By the next morning, poor Passepartout knew he needed to eat soon. He could sell his watch, but it was very special to him. He didn't really want to part with it. After much thought, he decided to try and sing for his supper.

But I am too well dressed for street singing, he thought. *I know, I'll trade my clothes for something more Japanese.*

He came out of the clothing dealer with a few pieces of silver in his hand and a brand-new Japanese costume. He wore a long coat and a one-sided turban.

I can pretend I'm in a carnival! he thought.

Passepartout entered the first teahouse he came upon. Once he sat down, he ordered some rice with chicken and ate it very quickly. During his meal he thought that maybe he could find a job on a steamer bound for America instead of singing for food or money.

He thought, *That way I have at least a hope of finding the monsieur!*

Passepartout walked back down toward the wharf. *How will I find a job? Who will let me on board dressed as I am?* These and other questions were rolling around his head when

89

he came upon a clown carrying a large billboard.
It said—

ACROBATIC TROUPE

PRESENTED BY THE

HONORABLE

WILLIAM BATULCAR

DON'T MISS THE LAST

SHOW OF THE

LONG NOSES! LONG NOSES!

WE ARE HEADING TO

AMERICA!

"Going to America!" Passepartout said.
"That's exactly what I need!"

He followed the clown back into the heart of
the city. Fifteen minutes later, Passepartout
stopped in front of a large cabin decorated with
streamers and painted to show a scene of jugglers.
Passepartout went inside and asked for Mr.
Batulcar, who came right out.

"What do you want?" he asked the butler.

"I am a gymnast, a singer, and a performer, sir. Do you have any need of my skills?" Passepartout asked.

"You are a Frenchman?" Mr. Batulcar asked.

"Yes. I am from Paris, but I have been living in England for many years. Now I would like to see America," Passepartout said.

"Are you strong?" Mr. Batulcar asked. "Can you sing standing on your head with a top spinning on your left foot and a sword balanced on your right?"

"Humph!" Passepartout replied, "I think so!" He remembered how nimble he used to be in his younger days. In fact, he used to be an acrobat!

"Well, that's good enough for me. You're hired!" He looked at Passepartout. "But you'll have to find something half-decent to wear. That costume you have on looks silly."

Passepartout was happy to have something to

do at last. If he couldn't be Mr. Fogg's butler, at least he could make his way to America and find him there. It was decided that he would become a Long Nose. They were a special act within the troupe that formed a human pyramid. This great attraction was the final act of each show.

The crowd started to gather in the afternoon. People of all different shapes, sizes, and colors filled up the stands. The musicians were there, too. They were playing their gongs, tamtams, flutes, drums, and tambourines.

The acrobats jumped into action. They rolled, bounced, jumped, and dove—much to the delight of the crowd. There was a juggler who threw lit candles into the air! He would blow them out as they passed by his mouth, and then light them again without ever dropping one. Tightrope walkers crossed thin wires across the stage. They twirled and jumped without falling.

The main attraction, though, was the Long

Noses. They were all dressed like the ancient god Tingou, who had a very long nose. They also had a splendid pair of wings. Their noses were made of bamboo and were five, six, even ten feet long! Some were straight, some were curved, and some had funny warts on them. The acrobats rolled and tumbled with these noses on their faces. It was quite incredible to see.

Mr. Batulcar announced the very last act, the human pyramid. But instead of climbing on one another's backs, the performers were to balance on one another's noses! Passepartout stood in the center of the ring with his six-foot long nose attached to his face and multicolored wings on his back.

At least I'll be able to have some supper, he thought as he climbed atop a nose and did his best to balance.

But then, as quickly as they formed the pyramid, they all tumbled to the ground. Noses came crashing down all around.

Passepartout exclaimed, "My monsieur! You're here!" It was true! Phileas Fogg was sitting in the audience. He and Aouda had walked by the sign for the show as they were exploring the city and had decided to go inside and watch.

"Passepartout," he said, "is that you?"

"Yes! I'm here! I'm here!"

"Well," said Phileas, "let's get to that steamer, young man!"

Phileas, Aouda, and Passepartout left the theater and walked outside. Mr. Batulcar chased them outside, screaming about how Passepartout had ruined his Noses! Mr. Fogg kindly gave him some money to pay for the repairs and the three made their way to the steamer bound for America. There was just one thing. Passepartout had forgotten to take off his own nose. He wore it and his wings right on board the ship called the *General Grant*!

CHAPTER 13

Mr. Fogg and Party
Cross the Pacific Ocean

⌒

The trip from Japan to America was supposed to take twenty-one days, with the ship arriving in San Francisco on the second of December. The trip from San Francisco to New York should take nine days. This left ten full days to get back to London by the deadline. If Phileas was at all worried, he certainly didn't show it.

By the ninth day on board the ship, Phileas Fogg had traveled exactly one half of the globe. Now, with only twenty-eight days left, he needed to cross the other half!

Meanwhile, Detective Fix had finally gotten his arrest warrant. It had been waiting for him when he arrived in Japan. In fact, it had been on board the *Carnatic*, the steamer he was supposed to be on. Of course, the arrest warrant was useless now that Phileas was on his way to America. If he was no longer on British soil, Fix had no authority to arrest him.

"Well," Fix steamed, "it will still be good in London. I know for a fact that Phileas Fogg will have to return to his own country at some point."

Fix decided to follow Phileas until the bitter end. He holed himself up in his cabin on the *General Grant* so they wouldn't know he was on board. He didn't want to see Passepartout and have to explain what he was doing there.

But he couldn't stay inside all the time. One day he simply needed some fresh air. What a mistake that was! The moment he stepped out on deck, there was Passepartout. The butler walked right up to Fix and punched him on the nose. Fix fell down.

"Are you quite finished?" he asked, holding his nose.

"For the time being—yes," Passepartout answered.

"Then let me have a word with you," Fix said. "It's about your boss, please."

Passepartout agreed, although he still didn't trust the detective. Fix stood up and the two men went and sat on the deck chairs.

"So now you know my monsieur is an honest man," Passepartout said. "And you've given up this crazy idea that he is the bank robber?"

"Of course not," Fix said. Passepartout raised his fist again. "Wait! Let me finish." The butler lowered his hand. "I am now in the game. You see, the only way I can arrest him is if he's in

England. The only way to get him to England is for you to finish this crazy race around the world. I know I can't stop him, so I'll do what I can to help."

Passepartout said nothing, so Fix continued. "Are we friends?"

"No, we are not friends. But we can be allies. I should warn you, though. I will wring your neck at the first sign of you acting up like you did in Hong Kong!"

"Agreed," Fix said. He knew when he was beat.

Eleven days later, the *General Grant* docked in San Francisco. Phileas Fogg had not gained or lost a day—and he noted so in his journal.

Phileas went directly to the train station to find out when the next train left for New York City. It was at six o'clock, which meant that he and Aouda could rest at the International Hotel for the rest of the day.

While Passepartout ran some errands, Phileas and Aouda ate a lovely breakfast. Then, as he had done in every other port, Phileas went to the office to have his passport stamped. This time there were no mishaps and everyone, including Fix, boarded the train for New York City at exactly six o'clock that night.

❧

Inside the train the weary passengers fell asleep. It had been dark by the time the travelers boarded the train, so there wasn't much to see out the window anyway. The train sped through California. It passed by Sacramento and started through the Sierra Nevada Mountains. The tracks wound in and out of the passes and the smoke from the train drifted through the giant trees.

After breakfast the next morning, the four passengers stared out the window at the great landscape before them. Mountains lined the horizon just beyond the prairies. Before long, Phileas began once again to write in his journal, as calm as he had ever been on this trip.

Just before lunch, a herd of buffalo found its way onto the tracks. The train stopped as the engineer waited patiently for them to pass. Passepartout couldn't sit still. He paced up and down the cars, wondering why someone didn't get out and make them move!

By evening on the second day, they had passed into Utah. They were near the Great Salt Lake, where the Mormons had settled.

The weather was very cold when Passepartout stepped outside for a breath of fresh air the next morning. It hadn't stopped snowing, but the sun was shining. The train sped by ranches and fields that would have grown wheat and corn had it been the right season. Now the ground was covered in a light dust of snow. Passepartout stretched his arms high above his head and thought, *This certainly is an interesting country.*

That afternoon the train stopped in Ogden. It was set to leave again in six hours. This meant that the travelers had time to explore Salt Lake City. A clay and pebble wall surrounded the city. It had been built in 1853. The travelers roamed around the streets. They looked at the square houses and then made their way back to the train.

Just as the whistle blew and the wheels started to turn, Passepartout looked out the window to see a tall man wearing a long, dark coat racing down the platform.

"Stop! Stop!" he yelled. Of course, the train couldn't stop. The man ran faster and faster, and then finally jumped on the rear platform. Passepartout smiled and thought to himself, *Maybe that man's making a tour of the world, too!*

～❀～

The train traveled north from Ogden, toward the Rocky Mountains. Passepartout paced up and down and had a hard time sitting still. Fix didn't like traveling through the mountains either. It scared him a bit. Of course, Phileas was perfectly calm—as was his nature.

It was still snowing. *Why didn't the monsieur take this trip in the summer?* Passepartout wondered. *Then we wouldn't have bad weather to deal with.* He looked out the window and thought about how gray the sky looked.

"These are long and slow hours to pass on the train," Fix said.

"Yes," said Phileas, "but they do pass."

"We could play cards," Fix suggested.

"Grand idea!" Phileas replied. "Let's play some bridge."

And so the group passed many hours in just

that fashion—playing cards, chatting with one another, and eating breakfast, lunch, or dinner. Phileas was right—the time did pass.

⌒

Suddenly a very loud whistle sounded and the train came to a complete stop.

"Passepartout, please go and see what happened," Phileas said.

Passepartout rushed out of the car. A group of other passengers had already gathered. A red light had stopped the train just before a bridge. The engineer and conductor were talking with the signal man about why he had stopped them.

"The bridge is out," he called up to them. "There's no way to pass."

The man in the long black coat, whose name was Colonel Proctor, said, "We're not staying here, are we? Taking root in the snow?"

"Of course not," the conductor said. "We've

telegraphed ahead for another train to meet us at Medicine Bow in six hours."

"Six hours!" Passepartout cried. "Six hours!"

"Yes," the conductor continued, "it will take that long for us to reach there on foot."

"On foot!" Passepartout said. "How far is this Medicine Bow?"

"It's only a mile from here," Colonel Proctor said. "Why would it take us six hours to get there?"

"Well, it's on the other side of the river," the conductor said.

"And we can't cross in a boat?" the colonel asked.

"That's impossible," the conductor replied. "The river is overflowing because of the rain. We have to walk ten miles north to be able to pass."

The passengers were all very upset at the idea of having to walk over ten miles in the wet, the cold, and the snow. The colonel was silent for a minute. Then he spoke up over the rest of the people, who were too busy complaining.

"Wait," he said. "I think there's a way we can get over the bridge."

"What do you mean?" the conductor asked.

"I think we have a chance of getting over if we push the train to its top speed," the colonel answered. "If we're at full speed, we might just make it before the bridge falls apart completely."

The passengers and the engineer were excited to try. They were all convinced that the plan would work and that they would make it across. If anyone was worried about the bridge collapsing first, they didn't say. Passepartout was a bit scared, but he didn't voice his fears. Everyone climbed back on board. Soon the train was moving again.

The locomotive whistled and drove into action. It sped faster and faster. In fact, it moved so fast that it felt like the train might not even be on top of the tracks! And then it passed over the bridge! The entire fateful trip took but a second as the train leaped from one bank of the river to the other. Just seconds after it was all over, the bridge fell with a crash into the water below.

CHAPTER 14

Phileas and Passepartout Meet Outlaws and Bandits on the Railroad

つ

The train took them past Fort Saunders and across the Cheyenne Pass to the Evans Pass. Here Phileas and Passepartout rode at the highest elevation since starting their incredible journey around the world. The train kept moving. It went through the territories of Wyoming and Colorado, and into Nebraska. As the train drove on, the four passengers passed the time playing cards.

Just as the train was making its way toward Omaha, there was a loud crash. The train stopped dead on the tracks. Each of the passengers in the car looked outside, but they couldn't see anything. Then, suddenly, the train started moving again.

"Now what on earth could have happened?" Passepartout asked. He looked over to Phileas and said, "I'm on my way, monsieur."

Passepartout stepped out of the car and walked toward the front of the train. A number of other men had come out of their cars as well, including Colonel Proctor. They could hear loud noises coming from one side of the train. Then people started screaming.

Back in the car, Aouda turned very pale. She heard the shouts and the noise from outside. "What do you think it is?" she asked.

Detective Fix replied, "I'll bet outlaws have attacked the train!"

Phileas calmly put his cards down. "If that is the case, we might have a fight on our hands!" He saw the shocked look on Aouda's face and said, "But let's hope it does not come to that," he said. "Aouda, you must stay here and keep safe. Lock that door and don't let anyone in!"

As it turned out, a gang of close to one hundred men had attacked the train. Many of them had jumped on board while the train was still moving! They were armed with guns and wore handkerchiefs over their faces. They had taken over the engine car and knocked the engineer out cold. Moving from car to car, they were taking whatever they could from the poor travelers.

The train drove faster and faster with no engineer to control it. If it wasn't stopped, the train would most certainly crash. When Passepartout discovered what was going on, he and Colonel Proctor raced back to help fight. Many of the men on board were already battling with the bandits. Passepartout dove right in, punching and kicking, and using all of his acrobatic abilities. Colonel

Proctor had a very strong punch and knocked a few of the bandits out with his bare hands!

In the fray, amid arms and fists flying, Passepartout noticed three bandits ganging up on the poor conductor. As the conductor fell to the ground, he shouted, "Unless the train is stopped at Fort Kearney, we will all surely die! The train will crash! The train will crash!"

By this time, Phileas had joined the fight. In fact, he was right beside the conductor. He punched a wayward bandit on the nose and said, "It shall be stopped then!" He started to rush toward the front of the train, but Passepartout stopped him. "Stay, sir! I will go."

Phileas did not have time to stop him. Another bandit jumped on his back and started to pull him down.

Passepartout slipped out of the car and crawled under the moving train. Using his experience as an acrobat, he held onto chains, pulled himself along by the brakes, and crept from one car to the next until he reached the engine.

Working as hard as he could, Passepartout managed to pull the safety chain from the engine car. He watched as the engine pulled away from the rest of the train and then worked the brakes as best as he could. Finally the rest of the train came to a stop right in front of the Fort Kearney station. The engine car rode off into the distance by itself.

The soldiers from the fort had heard the commotion and were ready to fight the bandits. But when the band of rascally men saw the soldiers lined up with their guns ready to fire, they abandoned the train. They jumped back on their horses and sped off.

Once they determined that it was safe, Aouda, Phileas, and Fix got off the train and stood on the platform. "Where is Passepartout?" Aouda cried. "He's not here!"

Phileas tried to comfort her, but he knew what she and Fix were thinking—Passepartout had been taken by the bandits! Aouda started to weep.

If his butler was a prisoner of the outlaws, Phileas had to save him. There was no other choice.

"Don't worry, Aouda," he said. "I will find Passepartout, alive or dead."

"Oh, Phileas!" she cried, covering her face with her hands.

"Alive!" he insisted, "if we get going right now." Phileas turned around and saw the captain of the fort standing nearby. "Captain!"

The man turned to him. "Sir," Phileas said, "my butler has been taken by the bandits. I would imagine they have taken other passengers as well. We must go after them!"

"That is a very serious thing to do, sir," the captain said. "They may ride all the way back to

Arkansas, and I can't leave the fort without protection."

"Very well then," Phileas said. "I will go alone."

"Alone!" Fix shouted. "You're going to chase the bandits by yourself?"

"No, I won't hear of that," the captain said. "I'll give you thirty volunteers." He turned toward his troops. "Men! I need thirty of you to go with this brave man to rescue the passengers the bandits have kidnapped. Who will go?"

The entire company stepped forward. The captain chose thirty of his best men. Soon they were ready to go.

"I'm coming with you," Fix insisted.

"No," Phileas replied, "you must stay with Miss Aouda, in case anything should happen to me—"

Fix put aside his feelings about Phileas and said, "Very well. I will stay." He turned to Aouda.

"Not to worry, Miss. Colonel Proctor is also here with us." The colonel was sitting down tending to a wound on his arm. When he saw them looking at him, he gave a triumphant wave with his good hand.

Phileas squeezed Aouda's hand and left her in charge of his carpetbag. Then he joined the soldiers. They had found a spare horse for him to ride. Before leaving, he said to the soldiers, "My friends, I want to get our fellow passengers back alive. To make it worth your while, I will divide five thousand dollars among you after we save these prisoners."

And with that, they were off!

❧

While Aouda waited patiently inside the station for Phileas and the soldiers to return, Detective Fix paced up and down. Suddenly a loud whistle was heard in the distance. What could it be? A dark shape came out of the snow. It was the locomotive! The engineer had woken up and discovered what had happened. He had driven the car backward all the way to Fort Kearny.

The passengers were very happy to see the engine. Now they could be back on their way to Omaha.

Aouda rushed out of the station. She asked the conductor, "Are you going to start?"

"At once, ma'am," he replied.

"But the prisoners—they are not back yet," she said. "We must wait for them."

"I'm afraid that's not possible. We must get going right away. We're already three hours behind schedule."

"I will not go," she said. "And you shouldn't either. It's shameful."

"I'm sorry you feel that way madam, but we have all the other passengers to think about as well," he said.

The other passengers—some wounded, some not—climbed on board and got back in their cars. Aouda bid good-bye to the colonel, who had decided to carry on with his trip. She thanked him for all of his help with the bandits.

Detective Fix stepped on board, too. But then at the last minute he decided to stay with Aouda, as he had promised. Steam blew out of the top of the train as it pulled away. It was still snowing.

Evening fell and still the prisoners hadn't returned. Aouda paced the length of the platform. Fix sat there as still as he could. As the sun set, the weather turned very cold. Aouda's imagination carried her far away. What could have happened to Phileas and Passepartout?

At dawn, a signal shot was heard in the distance. Aouda rushed out to the platform. Fix stood beside her. They were on the way back! Passepartout and Phileas were safe!

When they got back to the station, Phileas

handed out the reward to the brave soldiers who had helped him. Passepartout looked around for the train. His monsieur's trip was the most important thing on his mind.

"Where's the train?" he asked.

"Gone," Aouda said. "It left yesterday without us."

Passepartout cried, "It can't be! When will the next one come?"

"Not until this evening," she answered.

"Ah," Phileas Fogg said quietly.

Passepartout was very upset. The scuffle with the bandits could cost his monsieur the bet! "What shall we do now?" he asked.

No one said a word. No one knew what to do. They couldn't possibly wait for the train, but was there another way?

As much as he hated to do it, Detective Fix spoke up. He had made a promise to help Passepartout keep his boss on the right track and

the sooner they got back to England, the sooner
Fix could arrest him. "I might have a way," Fix
said. Everyone looked at him. "Last night a man
spoke to me of a sled with sails that could take us
to Omaha. We could catch up with the train to
New York there."

"There is hope then!" Passepartout exclaimed.

"Let's see what he has to say," Phileas said,
"this man with the strange sled."

～

The man who owned the sled was called Mudge.
During the winter, his sleds would often carry
people from one train station to the next in bad
weather. The strange contraption was very tall. It
had a high mast that held the sail. There was
enough room to hold six people.

Phileas quickly made a deal with Mudge to
take them to Omaha. Not wanting Aouda to have
to travel in the open air, he asked if she wanted to

wait for the train. Passepartout could stay behind with her. She refused. Passepartout was glad to hear this. He still didn't trust the detective and wasn't eager to leave him alone with the monsieur.

It wasn't long before the sled was ready. Everyone climbed on board and tucked themselves in under blankets to keep warm.

What a journey! The sled sped over the prairie as lightly as a boat on the water. But it was freezing! The wind blew strong and in just the right direction. The great white fields in front of them never gave way to houses, towns, or villages, so there was nothing in their way. Every now and again they would pass a tree with not a single leaf on its branches.

Suddenly Mudge saw some white roofs in the distance. "We're there!" he shouted. The last few miles sped by and soon the travelers were racing to catch the train. They just made it!

They arrived in Chicago with just twenty-four hours to go before the steamer left for England. Like a flash, they sped onward. Finally New York came into view. The train stopped right in front of the steamer's office. The *China*, the steamer bound for Liverpool, had left just forty-five minutes before!

Passepartout was crushed. It couldn't be! They had come all this way only to miss the ship by three quarters of an hour.

"There's nothing to be done tonight." Phileas Fogg said. "Let's get a hotel. We'll figure out what to do next in the morning."

CHAPTER 15

Phileas Fogg Finds
a Way to Liverpool

⌒

The next day, Phileas left the hotel by himself. He intended to find a ship to take them to Liverpool right away. It was now December 12. He had just nine days, thirteen hours, and forty-five minutes to go.

He walked up and down the riverside, but he could find no boat to take him. He had almost given up all hope when he saw a small trading ship set apart from the rest. The chimney on top of the boat was puffing steam. It was about to leave.

Phileas hailed a boat to take him out to the ship. Soon he found himself on board the *Henrietta*. The captain was on deck. He was fifty years old, with large round eyes, bright red hair, and a copper beard. His name was Andrew Speedy.

"Are you about to set off to sea?" Phileas asked.

"Yes. We leave for Bordeaux in an hour," Captain Speedy answered.

"Have you any passengers?"

"No passengers," Captain Speedy said. "We never take passengers. They get in the way."

"Is your ship very fast?"

"Oh, she's fast all right. As fast as they come," said the captain.

"Will you take me to Liverpool? Well, myself and three other passengers," Phileas asked.

"No."

"No?"

"No. I said we're going to Bordeaux, so we're going to Bordeaux," Captain Speedy insisted.

Phileas tried everything. He tried to buy the boat. He tried to pay the captain to take him, but all offers were refused. Until now, he had been able to buy his way around the world. This time money wasn't the answer.

"Will you take us to Bordeaux then, for two thousand dollars apiece?" Phileas asked.

Captain Speedy scratched his head. "There are four of you?"

"Correct," Phileas answered.

"Are you all ready to go?" Phileas nodded. "Fine," the captain continued. "We set off at nine. If you're here, we'll take you to Bordeaux with us."

This left Phileas just half an hour to race back to the hotel, gather up Aouda, Passepartout, and Fix, and then get back to the *Henrietta*. And Phileas

Fogg never even showed an ounce of nerves! All four travelers were back on board with seconds to spare. Passepartout felt a bit uneasy knowing how much money his monsieur was spending to make it back to London in time to win the bet. As for Fix, every time Phileas paid for something, he saw his reward fading away. After all, the money he was spending belonged to the bank. The more money the robber spent, the less he had to give back to the bank. And the less the bank recovered, the less his own reward would be. Those thoughts did not do much for his already low spirits.

By noon the next day, the *Henrietta* was sailing along nicely. Phileas Fogg stood on the bridge and looked out across the Atlantic Ocean. Meanwhile, Captain Speedy had locked himself away in his cabin. He was very unhappy indeed.

Phileas wanted to go to Liverpool and would stop at nothing to get there. He had told his story to the entire crew. Once they knew how far he

had already come, they decided to help him. They abandoned the captain's orders and put the ship on a new course—one bound for Liverpool.

The voyage went well for the first few days. They burned the coal and kept the *Henrietta* going at full steam. They had passed Newfoundland and were now out in the open seas. Passepartout had been keeping the sailors company by performing for them. His good humor put everyone in a happy mood.

Aouda spent much of her time on deck with Phileas trying to calm her down. She was truly worried about how everything would turn out.

Suddenly the weather turned. The Atlantic Ocean was a very dangerous place to be in the winter. There were awful storms and wicked waves. A boat could be blown off course or overturned in an instant. Instead of sailing, they used only the engine. The coal was the only energy pushing them forward.

On December 16, the ship's engineer came on deck to tell Phileas that they were almost out of coal.

"Let me think about it for a minute," Phileas said to the man. The two stood in silence while he considered what to do next. "Keep the engines at full steam," he said. "I've got a solution. Passepartout!"

The butler jumped up from a lower deck and stood before him. "Please ask the captain to come out of his cabin." Passepartout nodded.

The captain did not want to budge. He was quite angry that Phileas Fogg had taken over his ship. He did not want to talk to the man, let alone go up on deck. But Passepartout insisted.

"Where are we?!" the captain barked.

"Seven hundred and seventy miles from Liverpool," Phileas replied.

"Pirate!" Captain Speedy yelled at him. "Sea-skimmer!"

"Sir," Phileas said, "I'm going to need to burn the top of the ship. We're almost out of coal."

"B-burn my s-s-hip?" Captain Speedy said. "Absolutely not!"

Phileas reached into his pocket and took out a very large roll of money. "Here is enough money to buy two more ships. It should make up for everything I have done to you and to this boat."

Captain Speedy took the money quietly. He forgot his anger and dropped any grudges he might have toward Phileas Fogg. *If this man is willing to spend everything he has to get to Liverpool,* Captain Speedy thought, *I might as well help him. There simply isn't anything else I can do. And two ships will make me a far better living than just one.*

"Consider the *Henrietta* yours, Mr., I mean, Captain Fogg," Speedy said.

Over the next few days, the crew burned parts of the ship to keep it going. With just over nine hours to go, they arrived at the port in Liverpool.

Phileas Fogg, Aouda, and Passepartout raced off the *Henrietta*. They left her with Captain Speedy and stepped onto British soil.

At that very moment, Fix came up behind them and put his hand on Phileas's shoulder.

"Are you really Phileas Fogg?" he asked.

"I am."

"Then I arrest you in the Queen's name," Fix said. He held the arrest warrant in his hand.

CHAPTER 16

The Bet Is Lost!

Phileas Fogg was in prison. He had been locked up at the Custom House since Fix had arrested him a few moments before. He was to be sent back to London in a matter of minutes.

When he saw Fix arrest his monsieur, Passepartout tried to attack the detective in a rage. But there were policemen by the detective's side and they held the butler back. Aouda was thunderstruck. She did not understand what was going on. Passepartout explained everything. He told her that Fix thought Phileas Fogg was the bank robber and described how he had chased them around the world.

Was this all my fault? Passepartout thought. *What if I had told the monsieur about Fix from the beginning? Could I have stopped him from being arrested? Maybe the monsieur would have been able to convince Fix of his innocence?*

But it was too late to do anything differently. Passepartout sat down at the Custom House and cried. Aouda was there, too. Neither one wanted to leave until they could see Phileas.

Phileas Fogg had no more chances left. He needed to be at the Reform Club in exactly nine hours. The trip from Liverpool to London would take six, but now that he was under arrest, there was no guarantee he would even make it to London in time to clear his name, much less get himself over to the Reform Club.

Inside his jail cell, Phileas Fogg sat very still. Although the bench was hard and his future uncertain, he was not emotional. He simply sat there, waiting. For what? Did he still hope to win the bet? Even with the prison doors closed in front of him, could he still win?

Phileas carefully set his watch down beside him and looked at the hands as they moved. He didn't say a word. The situation was this: if Phileas Fogg was honest, he was ruined. If he was the robber, he was caught.

Did he think about escaping? Maybe just once as he walked slowly around the cell. But the door was hopelessly locked and there were iron bars on the windows. He sat down and took his journal from his pocket. He wrote, "December 21, Saturday, Liverpool." Then he added, "80th day, 11:40 a.m." All he could do now was wait.

The Custom House clock struck one. His watch was two hours too slow! They must have lost time somewhere along the way. Phileas thought to himself that if he was on an express train, he could be in London and just make it to the Reform Club in time to win his bet. But alas, he was stuck in jail. Another hour and a half went by before he heard some noise outside. It was Passepartout. His eyes brightened just a bit.

The door swung open and Phileas saw Passepartout, Aouda, and Fix, who hurried toward him.

Fix was panting and his hair stood up on end. "Sir, s-s-i-r," he stuttered, "forgive me—there's been—mistake—he looked just like you—robber—he—h-h-e—was arrested a few days ago! You are free."

The real robber, James Strand, had been arrested in Edinburgh three days ago. Phileas Fogg was innocent! He stood up and straightened his coat. Then he walked quickly up to Detective Fix and promptly hit him on the nose. He knocked him right down!

"Well done, sir!" Passepartout said. Fix didn't move. He knew he had received what he deserved. Phileas, Aouda, and Passepartout left the Custom House in a hurry. They jumped into a cab and raced to the train station.

"Have we missed all of the trains to London?" Passepartout said to no one in particular.

"Let me find out!" Phileas said. He went to the ticket desk and asked if there was an express train leaving shortly.

"I'm sorry, sir," the clerk said. "It just left five minutes ago!"

"Oh, no!" Aouda said. "We'll never make it now."

"I've got an idea," Phileas said. "Let me see if I can hire a train to take us to London. Wait here."

Phileas spoke with the clerk, who called the station manager. The two men discussed the situation. A few minutes later, Phileas walked back over to Passepartout and Aouda.

"I've hired a special train. We're leaving at three p.m.," Phileas said.

At last the three world travelers were on the final leg of their journey. When Phileas Fogg stepped onto the platform in London, the clocks were striking ten minutes before nine. Having made it around the world in eighty days, he arrived just five minutes too late—he had lost the bet!

CHAPTER 17

The Bet Is Won!

⌒

The doors and windows of Phileas Fogg's house on Savile Row were all closed. The curtains were drawn. Nothing in the house suggested that he was home. He had been ruined by one silly detective. Ruined!

After traveling all that way and after overcoming danger and all the other bumps along the way, it was finished! He owed the rest of his fortune to his friends at the Reform Club. What little money he had left was in his carpetbag.

Phileas went to bed that night with a heavy

heart. Aouda did, too. She felt so bad for the kind man who had rescued her. But she didn't know what she could do to help him now.

The next morning when Passepartout brought up his breakfast, Phileas asked him to tell Aouda that he would see her after dinner. He needed to spend the day making sure his affairs were in order. No one felt worse than the faithful butler. He knew it was all his fault they had lost the bet. If he had just told the monsieur about the detective, things would have turned out differently.

Passepartout could hold his feelings in no longer. "But sir! Why aren't you mad at me? This is all my fault—"

"I don't blame anyone, Passepartout. Now go find Miss Aouda, please."

"Yes, sir." Passepartout went off to tell Aouda that Phileas wanted to talk with her after dinner.

For the very first time in a very long time, Phileas Fogg did not set out for the Reform Club at exactly half-past eleven. Why did he need to go? He was a day late. His friends already had the check. All they needed to do was go to the bank to cash it. So Phileas stayed at home. He stayed in his room and did a lot of thinking. Aouda did the same. It was only Passepartout who buzzed around that day from door to door, trying to hear if he was needed.

After dinner, Phileas and Aouda sat down to have their talk. "Aouda," he said, "will you forgive me for taking you to England? When—"

"What do you mean? You saved me!"

"Please let me finish," he continued. "I was a rich man when I brought you here, far away from your home. I could have helped you start a new life. Now I'm ruined."

"I know, dear Phileas," Aouda said. "But all I ask is that you forgive me for being a part of that ruin. It's my fault you had to rescue me in the first place."

"That's nonsense. You needed to be safe and now you are."

"That's true," she said. "But what will become of you?"

Phileas looked at the kind girl that sat in front of him. "I have no true friends and no family, but I'll be fine."

"Well," Aouda said, "if you'll have me as your wife, I'll be your family. We can face the future together."

Phileas stood up. He didn't know what to say. His eyes lit up and his lips trembled. Aouda said nothing. She just waited for him to speak.

"I do love you!" he said. "Yes, by all that is good and honest, I do love you! Let's get married." They held tightly to each other's hands.

Passepartout came into the room and saw the pair smiling

happily. Phileas said, "We're getting married! Do you think it's too late to talk to the Reverend at the Marylebone Parish?"

"You'd like to get married tomorrow, on Monday?" Passepartout asked.

"Yes, tomorrow," Phileas answered.

"Yes," Aouda echoed.

Passepartout ran off as fast as his legs would carry him.

⁓

Passepartout raced into the sitting room where Phileas and Aouda were waiting for him.

"Marriage—" Passepartout said, "impossible, tomorrow." He was out of breath.

"What are you talking about?"

"To-tomorrow is Sunday!"

"No, it's Monday," Mr. Fogg insisted.

"No, t-t-oday is Saturday," Passepartout said. He grabbed Phileas by his collar and pulled him along. They jumped into a cab. It was now eight-thirty on December 21, and Phileas Fogg had fifteen minutes to reach the Reform Club.

こ∽

Phileas Fogg's bridge partners sat in the grand hall at the Reform Club watching the clock. They looked at one another and tried to read the newspapers to pass the time. Of course, the only thing in the newspapers was Phileas Fogg, so it was hard to avoid the subject!

"Well, gentlemen," Thomas said, "Phileas has one quarter of an hour left before his time runs out. Do you think he'll make it?"

Andrew said, "If he had been on the seven twenty-three train from Liverpool, he would have been here already. I think we've won!"

"I don't think we should be too quick to count him out just yet," Samuel said. "Phileas always arrives exactly on time."

Thomas said, "But the fact remains, the entire trip was a bit of a gamble. Even a delay of just one day could have ruined his chances of getting back in time."

"He has lost, gentlemen. He has lost," Andrew insisted. "The only steamer he could have been on was the *China*, and I know for a fact he wasn't. My guess is that he's at least twenty days behind."

It was now eight-forty. "Only five minutes remain," Ralph said. "I guess Andrew will be cashing his check at the bank tomorrow."

The five gentlemen looked at one another. They were all nervous. They tried to pick up their cards and finish the hand, but no one could take his eyes off the clock.

The seconds started to count down, fifty, fifty-one, fifty-two. At fifty-five, a great noise followed by applause was heard outside. All five men stood up from their seats. At the fifty-seventh second,

Phileas Fogg opened the door of the grand room and said, "Here I am, gentlemen!"

Phileas Fogg had made it around the world in eighty days. He had won the bet. But how? Where had he lost a day? Especially for someone who kept such exact time. It seemed that Phileas and Passepartout had forgotten to consider the different time zones around the world. As they traveled east, they gained an hour here and there. By the time they got back to London—they had gained an entire day! If only their watches had marked the days instead of just the hours, they would have known this!

So Phileas had not lost his fortune and for this he was quite happy. But he did have one question. Would Aouda still marry him?

"I think *I* should ask the question," she said. "Now that you are rich again, would you still like to marry me?"

"My dear Aouda," he answered, "if it were not for you, I would not have any money at all. If you hadn't asked me to marry you, Passepartout never would have gone to see the Reverend—"

"Oh, dear Phileas," she said, "how wonderful you are."

⌒

Two days later, Phileas and Aouda were married. Passepartout continued to be their butler and was quite happy in his job.

Phileas Fogg had won the wager and made a grand tour around the world. He rode an elephant, bought a boat, took many trains, sailed on many steamers, and had a great adventure. And what had he gained for his trouble? Well, a wonderful woman who made him truly happy indeed, and isn't that just enough for any good man?

What Do *You* Think?
Questions for Discussion

⁓

Have you ever been around a toddler who keeps asking the question "Why?" Does your teacher call on you in class with questions from your homework? Do your parents ask you questions about your day at the dinner table? We are always surrounded by questions that need a specific response. But is it possible to have a question with no right answer?

The following questions are about the book you just read. But this is not a quiz! They are designed to help you look at the people, places, and events in the story from different angles. These questions do not have specific answers. Instead, they might make you think of the story in a completely new way.

Think carefully about each question and enjoy discovering more about this classic story.

1. Why do you suppose it is so important to Phileas that everything be exactly as he wants it? Do you know anyone who acts like this? Is there anything in your life that always has to be just right?

2. Why do you think Phileas agrees to make the trip around the world? Have you ever traveled? What part of the world would you most like to visit?

3. Fix says that one just knows when they're in the company of a bad man. Do you agree with this statement? Do your first impressions of people tend to be accurate?

4. Passepartout spends the trip through India marveling at the many animals he sees. What is the strangest animal you've ever seen? What is your favorite animal?

5. Why does Passepartout decide to join the Long Noses? Did you think he would do well? Have you ever been to the circus? What's your favorite act?

6. When Phileas offers to rescue Passepartout from the train bandits, the captain at Fort Kearny says to his men, "I need thirty of you to go with this brave man." Do you agree that Phileas is brave? What is the bravest thing you have ever done?

7. When the train conductor wants to leave without the passengers who were kidnapped, Aouda says, "I will not go. And you shouldn't either. It's shameful." Do you agree? What would you have done in the conductor's place?

8. Everyone tries to take responsibility for

Phileas arriving home late. Do you think it is actually anyone's fault? Have you ever accidentally ruined someone's plans? How?

9. In what ways is Passepartout different from Phileas Fogg? Which of the men are you more like?

10. The idea of time plays an important role in the book. How does it affect each of the characters? What role does time play in your life?

Afterword

by Arthur Pober, Ed.D.

෯

First impressions are important.

Whether we are meeting new people, going to new places, or picking up a book unknown to us, first impressions count for a lot. They can lead to warm, lasting memories or can make us shy away from any future encounters.

Can you recall your own first impressions and earliest memories of reading the classics?

Do you remember wading through pages and pages of text to prepare for an exam? Or were you the child who hid under the blanket to read with a flashlight, joining forces with Robin Hood to save Maid Marian? Do you remember only how long it took you to read a lengthy novel such as *Little Women*? Or did you become best friends with the March sisters?

Even for a gifted young reader, getting through long chapters with dense language can easily become overwhelming and can obscure the richness of the story and its characters. Reading an abridged, newly crafted version of a classic novel can be the gentle introduction a child needs to explore the characters and storyline without the frustration of difficult vocabulary and complex themes.

Reading an abridged version of a classic novel gives the young reader a sense of independence and the satisfaction of finishing a "grown-up" book. And when a child is engaged with and inspired by a classic story, the tone is set for further exploration of the story's themes, characters, history, and details. As a child's reading skills advance, the desire to tackle the original, unabridged version of the story will naturally emerge.

If made accessible to young readers, these stories can become invaluable tools for understanding themselves in the context of their families and social environments. This is why the Classic Starts series includes questions that stimulate discussion regarding the impact and social relevance of the characters and stories today. These questions can foster lively conversations between children and their parents or teachers. When we look at the issues, values, and standards of past times in terms of how we live now, we can appreciate literature's classic tales in a very personal and engaging way.

Share your love of reading the classics with a young child, and introduce an imaginary world real enough to last a lifetime.

Dr. Arthur Pober, Ed.D.

Dr. Arthur Pober has spent more than twenty years in the fields of early childhood and gifted education. He is the former principal of one of the world's oldest laboratory schools for gifted youngsters, Hunter College Elementary School, and former Director of Magnet Schools for the Gifted and Talented for more than 25,000 youngsters in New York City.

Dr. Pober is a recognized authority in the areas of media and child protection and is currently the U.S. representative to the European Institute for the Media and European Advertising Standards Alliance.

Explore these wonderful stories in our
Classic Starts™ library.